DAVID AND JACKO

THE ANT GOD

DAVID AND JACKO

THE ANT GOD

DAVID AND JACKO: THE ANT GOD

ISBN: 978-1-922159-43-4
Illustrated by Tea Seroya

Visit the author's website: www.davidjdownie.com

See other books by the Author at his Amazon author page:
www.amazon.com/author/bestsellers

Published by Blue Peg Publishing

If you have purchased the ebook version of this book, then please consider buying the beautiful print version if your family enjoys the ebook.

THE FLYING ANTS

They were all over me. Just irritating at first, all up and down my arms, and then my legs and my body. Biting me. I tried to brush them off, but my arms were trapped, and there were so many of them.

They were ants. On my face. Crawling in my ears. They started biting me all over as I clawed at them. Each bite stung like acid.

I woke up in sweaty terror. I was in my bed, and it was dark. I sat upright, but in my half-asleep state I wasn't sure what had happened. Common sense told me I had just had a horrible dream of getting eaten alive by ants.

I leaned over to the side of the bed and flicked on a lamp to try and settle myself.

My bed *was* full of ants! Writhing black masses of them, right where I was sleeping. It hadn't been a dream after all. I was being eaten alive!

I jumped out of bed as quickly as I could and ran down the hallway, petrified, feeling like an animal must feel when it is in danger of being eaten by another animal.

I took a moment down the hallway to compose myself. Jacko, my little dog, had followed me from just outside my bedroom. He looked bemused, and I scratched him on the head to distract myself.

"Come on mate," I said. "That was pretty awful. What the hell were those ants doing in my bed?"

Jacko just looked at me. He didn't seem too convinced.

I wandered back down the hallway, slowly, with Jacko close behind. I paused at my door to turn on my main light.

The bed was empty. There was not an ant to be seen.

I stood there, confused. It had seemed so real. Some of the bites were still stinging me, or so it seemed. Perhaps I was losing my mind.

I had better not tell my parents, I thought, as I turned the room light off and moved back towards my bed. Thankfully my bed lamp was still on. I planned to keep it on, as I was still a bit shaken.

As I got closer to the bed and was about to hop in, I noticed two or three little black shapes on the mattress when I moved the sheet.

What the . . . ?

Perhaps they had caused me to have that horrible dream, I thought. I peered at them closer. They looked like ants, but they had wings.

Ants don't have wings, I thought to myself. Or do they?

Just as I was pondering this, the ants took off into the air and flew outside my window.

Jacko and I just looked at each other in shock for a moment before I closed my window up tight and tried to sleep for the rest of the night with the light on.

TROUBLE IN ANTLAND

When I finally got up, I was both grumpy and disturbed. That didn't bother Dad, though, who was doing something out in the backyard that involved a lot of noise.

Bang, bang, bang!

He was hammering something, which was just what I needed after my poor night's sleep. Granddad had given me a tiny hammer as a toy when I was little, but the first thing I hammered was our new TV. Mum still liked to point out the chips in the glass when guests came over.

It was when Dad found me hammering nails into the power point that he took the hammer away from me, and I have stayed away from carpentry ever since.

"Bloody ants!"

Dad was talking to himself, but this got my interest. What trouble was he having with ants after my little adventure during the night, I wondered.

I went out to the backyard through the hole in the wall where the fireplace used to be, and Dad looked up from his workbench.

"Look at these bloody things," he said, pointing to a line of black ants coming out of various places in the garden and passing right by him.

"They started crawling over my foot," he said. "Little beggers."

It was quite the sight. It would seem that all the ants of our garden were coming out of their hiding places—the drains, the gardens, under the barbeque—and heading off together for some sort of adventure.

"Ants move sometimes when it rains," said Dad. "But I've never seen anything quite like this."

Neither had I. It was weird all right, but I didn't have any more time to think about it as I was late for school. I grabbed my bike from around the side of the house and headed off on my normal route. Jacko followed, which he did sometimes, even though he strictly wasn't meant to and he sometimes got locked up in a cage by the school janitor.

After a while it became clear that the ant issues weren't confined to our backyard or my bed. There were little black streams coming out of every house, where they joined up to the main stream, which was getting quite crowded. It was like a road network of ants, all joining up to the highway during peak hour.

And by the looks of things, that highway was heading towards the trees around the school.

I wondered if a big storm was coming.

Class was normal enough. We had Mrs Bryce again as our teacher, and she laughed and asked us to write stories that were dark and funny at the same time. I wrote about a faraway land with creatures that lived by sucking out the eyes of flies.

I think she liked it.

It had gotten weird by the time I went to lunch though. The streams of ants seemed to have made it right into the school grounds. They were everywhere. A few of the kids were stomping on them and laughing, which I did think was pretty funny, although not as funny as the one kid who accidently ate an ant sandwich, and the other kid who literally got ants in his pants.

We probably squashed about 10,000 of them as we went down to the oval to play some soccer.

There weren't too many ants down there, though, so we had no problem starting our game. One of the teachers, Mr Motcher, took it upon himself to referee and was doing a pretty good job until he blew the whistle while I was running up field in a magnificent solo effort and was about to score.

"What is it, Mr Motcher?" I said, really disappointed.

Mr Motcher grabbed the ball from the ground and lifted it to his chest.

An ant ran out of one nostril and up the other.

It was quite repulsive.

"You, young man, touched the ball with your hands."

I protested my innocence as another ant pushed its way out of the edge of Mr Motcher's left eye. He didn't seem to notice—either the ants *or* my pleas for the ball.

By now I had had enough. I swung my foot hard up towards the ball, determined to continue my way up the field and score the goal that I had been wrongfully denied.

Really hard.

Unfortunately, rather than striking the ball out of Mr Motcher's hands, my foot came up short and I . . . hit Mr Motcher instead. Really, really hard. In a place where he didn't want to be hit. No, not at all.

It was an accident. But Mr Motcher didn't seem to see this. Instead, he yelped and immediately collapsed on the soccer field in a tight ball of pain.

"Downie," he whispered, with ants spilling out of his mouth and onto his chin, "you're going to pay for this. All of you kids. You're going to pay for this, I promise."

He licked the ants back into his mouth and looked pleased with himself.

By now Jacko had run out and joined us in the middle of the oval. He was yelping and quite agitated. "Yes, yes mate," I said. "I know, it isn't fair, but he's the teacher. I shouldn't have kicked him, especially there."

Jack yelped some more, which caused me to look up from Mr Motcher, who was still lying on the ground.

There was a black wall about a foot high making its way over from the playground onto the oval. Towards me. It was black, like the ant stream on the ground, except it was surging, like a wave at sea, and coming forward across the grass quite quickly.

If I didn't know any better, I would have said it was a wall of ants.

Mr Motcher started laughing from the ground. Ants dropped out of his mouth and onto the grass as he did so.

"Downie, I told you you were going to pay."

How was this possible? I didn't want to stay to find out. I started running towards the edge of the oval. There was another layer of ants on the school ground that also seemed to be growing in size and becoming more agitated.

By now, other children had noticed and were starting to panic. One had tripped over and, within seconds, was screaming and covered with ants.

I didn't have time to stop. It was getting harder and harder to run because the ants made it slippery. I had to pick up Jacko, or his little paws would have been covered with them.

We made it to our classroom and locked the door behind us. Exhausted, I paused for a moment to recover my breath. The room was empty except for Mrs Bryce, who was by the window and looked a deathly pale colour.

Wordlessly, she held up her arm to point outside.

Ant chaos reigned. The black, swarming mass was everywhere. Students and teachers were covered in ants, screaming for their lives. One boy had lifted himself up on a monkey bar, but his dangling feet were red raw and being attacked by what must have been thousands of ants, each taking a tiny bite out of him.

Another boy from sixth grade had tripped and was immediately swarmed upon by the moving floor of ants. There were frantic movements for about thirty seconds, his arms and legs going in every direction, but eventually he was still. There was no sign of him shortly after that. He had just been swallowed up by the blackness.

The boy on the monkey bar was in a bad way. His screams made me look at him again, but I wished that I hadn't. He was still hanging on, but I could see parts of the bones of his feet. The ants were munching the flesh off bit by bit while he screamed and held on for his life.

"That's Mark. I taught him last year," said Mrs Bryce, who was clearly still in shock.

I opened a louver and yelled.

"Mark, mate! Hang in there buddy. We'll come and get you!"

Mark's screams tapered off all of a sudden, and he just hung there limply. I had read once about a fellow who was on the outside of a plane when it took off, and he had to hang on to the landing gear for hours or he would have fallen to his death. Apparently when he landed, he couldn't let go. Every ounce of his being had gone into locking his arms, and they stayed locked even when he passed out because of a lack of oxygen.

Perhaps Mark was like that now.

The ants had largely dropped off him, probably because there was nothing left to eat on his feet. They had been completely stripped of flesh, and you could see his white bones, which were being licked clean by four or five stragglers who clearly relished their task, and come to think of it, looked a little plump, for ants.

All of a sudden, the writhing blackness that covered the playground like a thick blanket was still. There was silence. No ant moved. Mark quietly swung back and forth on the monkey bar, footless.

Then there was the sound of rustling leaves and broken twigs. It started softly but got louder and louder. It seemed to be coming from the oval.

Mrs Bryce gasped. Approaching the classroom was Mr Motcher, arms folded as he stood high off the ground on a moving platform of ants like a magician on a magic carpet. He looked smug.

Jacko whined in fear.

THE ANT GOD

Mr Motcher floated towards us on his moving platform of ants. As he got closer, I could see how hundreds of thousands of them had locked to form a solid block that was, in turn, supported by millions of tiny black specs, all working together as one.

Mr Motcher paused outside the classroom, hovering, while the ants made the strange rustling sound we heard earlier. I could see more and more of them joining the bulk of the moving platform with every moment.

After pausing for what could only have been dramatic effect, Mr Motcher spoke.

"David, I can see you through the window, you know. You too, Mrs Bryce. And no doubt that little mutt, Jacko, is in there somewhere, cowering, which is to be expected from a creature more sewer rat than dog."

I looked down. Jacko *was* cowering. It wasn't fair to call him a rat though.

Mrs Bryce turned to me and whispered.

"I always knew this fellow wasn't right. I went to school with him, a million years ago. He had no friends then and doesn't now. And be beggared if he's getting an invite to this year's staff party."

"I heard that Mrs Bryce—or should I say, Rae?" Mr Motcher shouted from his ant platform.

I looked at my teacher. Rae?

Mr Motcher continued.

"It's not true to say I have never had any friends. *It's not true!* I have always had friends, *millions of friends*. Look around me, Rae. These are my friends. From the earliest of times, ants were my friends when nobody else wanted to be. They listened to me. They did what I said. *They still do what I say!*"

And with that, he rose higher into the air until he towered above us, the ants effortlessly supporting him. They were beyond counting now, just a limitless, seething, black mass that held him in the air and seemingly did his bidding.

He looked around at them all and brought his arms up triumphantly.

"My friends," he said.

"My friends *and* my children."

With that the ants climbed up onto their platform and headed towards Mr Motcher. Within moments they covered his legs, and then his torso, his outstretched arms, and even his face.

Mr Motcher was smothered in ants, no longer recognisable as human. He laughed. Even his teeth and tongue were covered with ants. It was freaky.

"And what should I have to complete the transformation, Rae? A sword?"

As he spoke, a black sword grew from his ant-covered hand until it was meters in length. If I hadn't known it was made from interlocked ants, I would never have guessed. It was formidable.

"Or perhaps a staff."

The sword transformed as he spoke into a long staff—the sort you would expect a wizard to have in a fairy story. He must have read a few because it even had a knobbly end on it.

"Yes, yes. A staff better suits me I think."

He peered down at us from his platform.

"It would be too easy to eat you alive. Too, too easy. I waited for decades as you ignored and disrespected me. Decades of quiet pain, with friends only in the dirt and darkness.

"No, each of you shall suffer some more, me thinks. Watch, as your town crumbles, and fear me. *Fear me!* Because I will be your end, before this week is out. Make no mistake about that."

He looked at me in particular.

"As for you, Downie. You will die screaming for your mother, for what you did to me today in front of the other children. But it will do you no good because she, too, will die a horrible death at my hand. You should know this, Downie, and reflect on your life of arrogance."

With that, he raised his staff of ants and, with a great surge, the platform on which he stood accelerated away. Whatever he was doing to control those ants made them move much faster than they did in my garden. And as he glided across the school grounds and out the front gate, every single ant went with him.

The schoolyard was quiet.

ANT CARNAGE

The devastation became apparent as the carpet of ants disappeared with Mr Motcher. Bodies of partially eaten students and teachers were scattered all over the playground. One boy was half buried in the sandpit, no doubt trying to escape the swarm by tunnelling head first into the sand.

His stripped leg bones were testament to the wisdom of his plan.

There were some who lived. Those that dived into the pool were fine as the ants had simply walked around the water. Others had climbed trees. Whether or not the ants followed seemed to have depended on whether or not Mr Motcher had seen them up there.

It seemed clear that it wasn't the ants that were at fault. They were just doing what Mr Motcher had told them to do.

Mark fell from the monkey bars, still unconscious and footless.

It was a house of horrors. Mrs Bryce puked without warning. All down her dress. It was all too much for me. She could call an ambulance to help the walking wounded. The others couldn't be helped at all.

I needed to get home to warn Mum and Dad.

Jack and I took off and I grabbed my bike. We passed one poor kid as we went out of the front of the school. He obviously had had the same idea but was now just a skeleton and a school uniform wrapped around a bike.

The ants must have caught him.

Ten minutes later I was back at Sabot Street. I must have been in time as Dad was out in front, digging some weeds.

"Hey matie," he said, obviously in a pretty good mood.

"Hi Dad," I replied. "Where's Mum?"

"She's just popped down to the Deli to grab some milk. How was school?"

They obviously hadn't heard. Dad was never much for watching TV during the day. I was worried about Mum. The problem with ants is that they are everywhere. If Mr Motcher wanted to find Mum, then he would have had no problem doing so.

"Back soon, Dad," I said as I peddled back down the street tracing Mum's steps. I went down the path between streets, crossed the road, and started on the second path down to the Deli when I saw Mum waving from the end of the path.

"Hi Davey," she yelled, smiling. She started jogging up towards me, which was pretty impressive for a mum. I relaxed and waited for her to arrive. We would have to go somewhere safe until we had solved the ant problem.

Further down the path, behind Mum, I could see a little movement of black. Perhaps these were stragglers looking for Mr Motcher, I thought.

But then the trickle of black became a gush. A river of ants came around the corner by the Deli and onto the path behind my mother. I screamed and Mum looked up, puzzled, before getting knocked down on her face from the weight of the river of ants.

“Noooooooooooooo,” I cried, knowing what this meant.

I jumped off my bike and ran towards Mum, who was now covered in a black, pulsating mess. That was it. She would be stripped by the time I got there, I thought, distressed.

"Mum, Mum!" I cried and bent down to the ants. I pushed handfuls of them to one side and felt around as best I could, fearing the worst.

Nothing. Then, meters away, Mum surfaced to the top of the dark wave. She was still alive! But she was being carried away from me, held off the ground by millions of tiny black feet. They were faster than you would think possible for ants, much faster than I could run.

They were obviously told to not harm her.

I ran back to my bike and jumped on. But by the time I had turned around and ridden down to the bottom of the path, Mum and the ants had vanished. Nowhere to be seen.

My mum was gone.

THE ZOO

I returned home. Dad was having a cup of tea.

"Where's your mother?" he asked. "We've run out of milk altogether."

I explained to Dad about Mr Motcher and the ants, as well as the carnage at the school. He took it pretty well until I told him about Mum. He wasn't happy about that.

"Well, we've got to find her!"

Dad is a very practical person. He immediately sat down with a map of Brisbane and tried to work out where he would have taken Mum if he were a deranged teacher with a fetish for ants.

He came up with three possible locations. One was on the top of Mt Cootha, where, according to Dad, a maniac with a god complex might go because of the view. The other was Southbank because it was central to everything. And then the third was a secret location he called "The Rock Park."

I knew of this place because Dad would drive there, and we would all hop out of the car and steal rocks for the garden, hoping we wouldn't get caught.

"Why would he want rocks?" I asked, confused.

"Not rocks!" said Dad. "Ant mounds. The place is full of them. If he wanted a good source of ants, then that would be where he would go."

We decided to split up. Dad would go to Mt Cootha and Southbank, with his old car. I wanted the Rock Park. It was the only place out of the three that made sense to me, plus I could get there on my bike.

But first I had to get supplies.

Dad dropped me at the hardware store, where I bought some goodies I put into my backpack. Next stop was, of all places, the local zoo.

Jacko looked at me as though I had gone bonkers.

The reception was empty. It was either a public holiday or the staff had been distracted by the carnage at the school. I jumped the main fence and made my way past the koalas and the kangaroos and the wombat, who looked very bored indeed, and then on to the enclosure I was looking for.

It was empty.

However, there was a tunnel at the back that had two entrances. We waited for about five minutes, but nothing happened.

"Watch this, Jack," I said and put my hand in my pocket.

"These little fellas are left over from the school."

I pulled out a handful of ants. Jack's eyes widened, and his mouth came up into an involuntary snarl.

"It's okay, mate," I said. "They're dead."

I cupped the ants in my hand and crouched down on my knees.

We watched the tunnel. After a minute or two, a very long nose appeared around the corner before an even longer tongue came out and snaffled a dead ant from the grass.

I could see Jack tense next to me.

The nose kept creeping out of the tunnel until it was followed by an elongated head and a big hairy body with a generous tail.

The creature's tongue kept darting in and out, licking up the trail of ants as it made its way towards me. Within moments it was right in front of me, clearly enjoying its feast and eating right out of my hand.

"He's been hungry, Jack," I whispered. "He hasn't had any ants to eat."

With that, I slipped one of Jacko's collars around the creature's neck and clicked on his lead.

Mr Motcher may have had 10 million ants on his side, but I had a hungry anteater on mine.

THE HOUSE OF ANTS

What a strange sight we must be, I thought to myself, as me, Jacko the dog, and a giant anteater made our way out of the zoo and towards the Rock Park. I was worried that the anteater would be unhappy, but it turns out he didn't like living in a small enclosure at a zoo very much at all. And he was hungry.

It took about 20 minutes to walk to the Rock Park. It was up a path through the trees just off the road. True to its name, there were a lot of rocks to be seen as well as ant hills, which is why we had come.

The anteater hurried over excitedly, but they were empty.

“Sorry, big nose,” I said, somewhat unkindly. “I think someone’s been here before us.”

And with that, we came to a ridge over which I could see the house.

It was black, all black, and like no house I had ever seen before. There were no doors, and I could see into the main room. Mr Motcher was sprawled back on a black couch, eating handfuls of what seemed like ants out of a big, black bowl. The ants that had covered his body were gone, but his ant staff was perched next to him. There was a second room attached to the first, and it was there that I imagined my mother was being kept.

We had found him!

I crept down the hills, carefully holding the anteater's lead. I don't think he could see Mr Motcher and his bowl of ants, but his giant nose was high in the air sniffing excitedly. He knew he was close to his dinner.

I didn't want the anteater charging ahead and ruining things, so I told Jacko to sit and had him bite the lead. I then crept around the side of the house and peered in the window to the second room. My mum was there all right, bound by black lashings of ant chains and gagged by a mouthful of them. She saw me in the window, and her eyes flicked back and forth, and she wriggled her head as though she was trying to tell me something.

"It's okay, Mum," I whispered. "We're going to get you out of here."

I crept back around the front of the house and carefully looked around the corner of the front door. Judging by the snores, Mr Motcher was asleep. I tiptoed in and made my way towards the second room. The floor squelched slightly under my feet, and I was almost there when I heard a voice.

"Mr Downie," said Mr Motcher, "I have been expecting you."

I turned and saw that Mr Motcher had woken up and was standing by his couch. He had grabbed his staff but didn't look nearly as formidable without his 10 million ants to help him.

"I'm sorry I kicked you," I said. "But this has gone too far. You have to let me take my mother back."

Mr Motcher looked at me. "I'm afraid that just isn't going to happen, little boy. Neither of you will leave this house today."

I looked at him again.

"Have you forgotten it was only this morning that I bested you on the school oval, Mr Motcher?" I said, feeling brave all of a sudden. "Do you want me to kick you again? Would you like that? You're not so scary without your ants, are you?"

Mr Motcher looked at me and laughed.

"Without my ants? Ah my boy. *I am never without my ants!*"

With that, he lifted his ant staff and his other arm high and appeared to concentrate. The house started shaking slightly, and I wondered what was going to happen.

"I am never without my ants, boy," he said, almost kindly.

Then the house collapsed. The walls drooped onto the floor, and the roof fell into pieces. Even the couch seemed to melt. I held my hands up over my head to protect myself, but I really didn't understand what was going on.

Within moments it was over. The house was all around me, and I could see Mr Motcher with his staff and my mother, who was still bound and surrounded by the black remnants of her room.

Mr Motcher lifted his staff even higher, and the black rubble became fluid, like at the school, and gushed over to where he was standing.

Oh no, I thought. The house was made of ants.

Mr Motcher was now surrounded by blackness, and it lifted him into the air on the platform as it had this morning. All of the ants from the house were with him now, and he looked quite pleased with himself.

He spoke quite deliberately.

"Now. You. Die."

He was raising his staff one last time when his platform started to shiver, and I heard a bark.

It was Jacko and the anteater.

The anteater was almost beside himself with pleasure and had started eating the corner of Mr Motcher's platform. Everywhere he went, the ants collapsed out of their formations and tried to run away from his darting tongue. Clearly their genetic fear of anteaters was at odds with their bizarre loyalty to Mr Motcher.

After a moment of shivering, Mr Motcher's platform collapsed and even his staff drooped. He fell awkwardly on the ground, and the ants started moving in every direction, his hold on them broken.

"Not so clever now, eh Mr Motcher?" I said as I made my way to my mother. Her bonds had broken with the arrival of the anteater, and she gave me a little hug, which was slightly embarrassing in the circumstances.

"It isn't over yet, boy," said Mr Motcher as he pulled himself off the ground. He walked a few meters away from the house and grabbed one of the rocks from what was, after all, the Rock Park.

He walked deliberately towards the anteater, who was having a feast for the ages, until Mr Motcher banged him on the head with the rock. I cringed for my hairy friend although I didn't think he was dead. He certainly wasn't awake.

Mr Motcher picked him up by his nose and held him up for the ants to see.

"Behold your ancestral foe!" he cried and threw the unconscious anteater away from the house. It lay upside down on the grass, clearly incapable of eating anything.

Obviously the ants agreed because within moments they had regrouped and swarmed back under Mr Motcher, who had returned to his platform. He held up his hand, and a thin, black line grew out of the seething mass and shaped into his staff.

He pointed the staff towards the inert anteater, and a branch of the platform broke off and moved towards him.

"No!" I cried. But it was too late—the swarm engulfed my furry friend in a black frenzy.

Time for plan B, I thought, as I reached into my backpack. The goodies I had purchased from the hardware store included four insect bombs for house fumigation, as well as some surface spray designed especially to kill ants.

I set the fumigations on, and they each sprayed their poison into the air. I held my breath, and Jacko ran for cover. I walked forward, an insect spray in each hand, spraying on the black clouds of ants as I went, and focussing on the swarm that had surrounded the anteater.

The ants did not fear the spray, but they should have. Within moments, millions of ant corpses were still, and Mr Motcher's platform collapsed again. The ants on my friend fell away to reveal a skeleton stripped to the bone.

I was too late and knelt down beside his remains. Even his long tongue was gone. It was terribly sad, and I shed a few tears thinking about what had happened. At least he was unconscious when he was eaten, I thought, as a rock smashed into the side of my head.

I woke moments later, groggy. I was sprawled next to the anteater skeleton. Mr Motcher stood above me, rock in hand.

"You think you can defeat me with fly spray?" he screamed. *"There are 10 quadrillion ants in the world, and you think you can beat me with fly spray?"*

With that, he held the rock up above his head and jumped in the air to body slam into my skull. In desperation I felt around and grabbed a large rib from the anteater skeleton and held it in front of me as he fell.

It skewered him through the chest, and the rock fell harmlessly to one side.

His body was on top of mine, and I pushed him off as he clutched the bone extruding from his chest and started spluttering blood. I picked up the rock he was going to kill me with and held it high above his head.

"This is for killing my anteater," I whispered, and dropped it.

Mum, Jacko, and I left Mr Motcher there with his millions of dead friends and walked the long walk home.

16101312R00032

Printed in Great Britain
by Amazon